Mem Fox

KOALA LOU

Illustrated by
Pamela Lofts

PENGUIN

VIKING

There was once a baby koala so soft and round that all who saw her loved her. Her name was Koala Lou.

The emu loved her. The platypus loved her.
And even tough little Koala Klaws next door
loved her.

But it was her mother who loved her most of all.
A hundred times a day she would laugh and shake
her head and say, 'Koala Lou, I DO love you!'

Whenever she stretched in the early morning sun, or climbed a gum-tree, or bravely went down the track all by herself, her mother would smile and say, 'Koala Lou, I DO love you!'

The years passed and other koalas were born –
brothers and sisters for Koala Lou. Soon her
mother was so busy she didn't have time to
tell Koala Lou that she loved her.

Although of course she did.

Every night, as she curled up under the stars, Koala Lou thought about the times when her mother had looked at her and said, 'Koala Lou, I DO love you!' and she longed for her to say it again.

One night Koala Lou had a splendid idea. Preparations had begun for the Bush Olympics. SHE would enter the Olympics! She would compete in the gum-tree-climbing event, and she would win, and her mother would fling her arms around her neck and say again, 'Koala Lou, I DO love you!'

Koala Lou began her training right away. She jogged and puffed, and lifted weights and panted. She hung from a branch with one claw at a time till she ached. She did push-ups till her stomach hurt, and last of all, she climbed the tallest tree that she could find, over and over and over again.

Sometimes her mother would watch her and ask, 'How're ya goin', blossom?'

'Fine, just fine,' Koala Lou would reply.

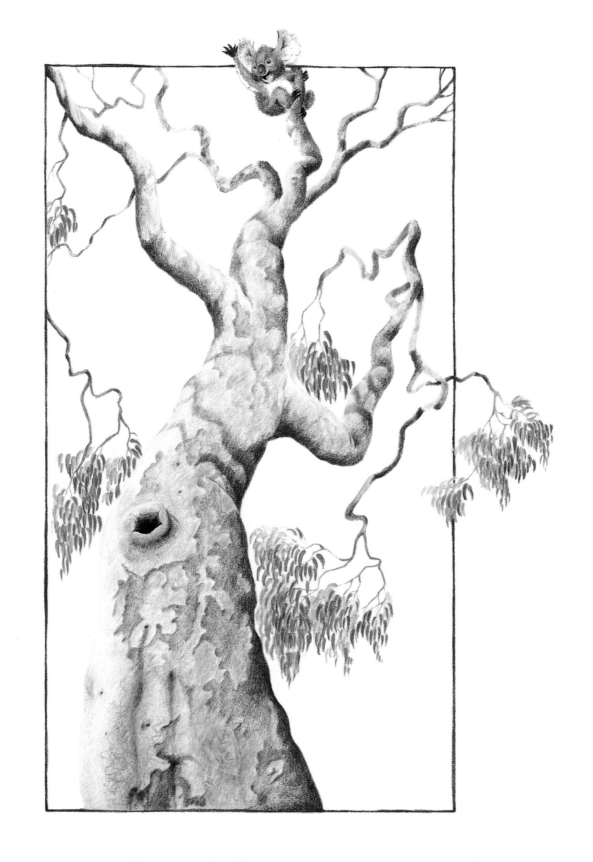

At last the day of the Bush Olympics arrived.

Koala Klaws had also entered the gum-tree-climbing and everyone knew how fast she was, but Koala Lou wasn't scared. She saw her mother in the crowd and imagined her saying again, 'Koala Lou, I DO love you!'

Her heart filled with hope.

It was Koala Klaws who went first.
Her climb was a record-breaking
twenty-two metres in seventy
seconds flat. The spectators whistled
and cheered and wildly waved their
holiday hats.

'Can I do better than that?' thought Koala Lou. 'I must.' As she stepped towards the tree, a hush fell over the crowd.

'On your mark,' said the kookaburra. 'Get set. GO!'

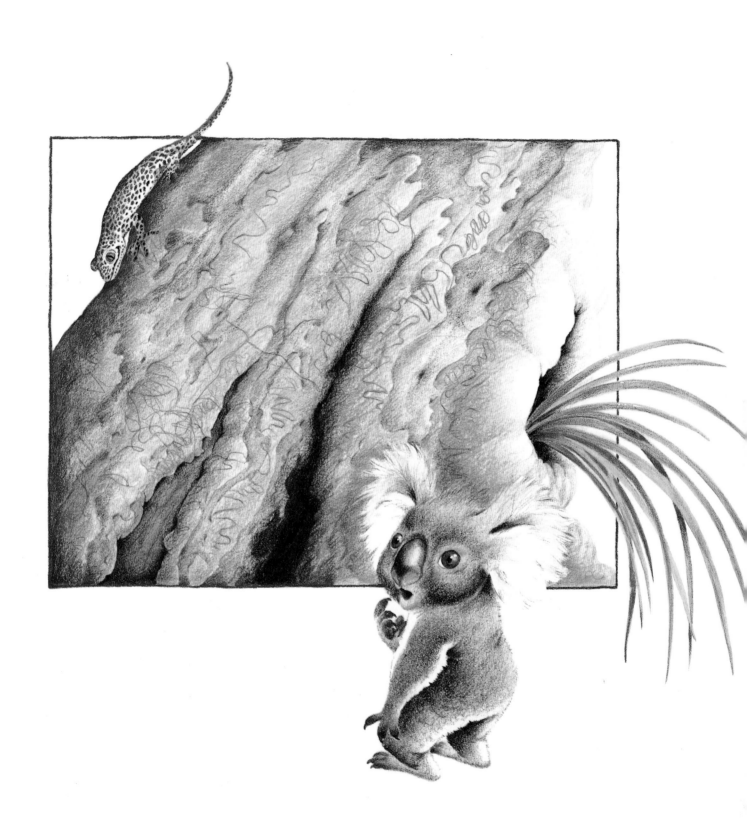

Koala Lou leapt on to the tree. Up and up and up she climbed – higher and higher and higher. Faster and faster and faster until – there she was, right at the very top! The spectators roared and clapped and stamped their feet.

But she wasn't fast enough. In spite of all her training and all her hoping, it was Koala Klaws who won the gum-tree-climbing. Koala Lou came second.

Koala Lou went off and hid. She heard the shouts of the Bush Olympics and cried her heart out.

When the first stars of evening appeared in the sky, Koala Lou
crept home through the dark and up into the gum-tree.
Her mother was waiting for her. Before she could say a word
her mother had flung her arms around her neck and said,
'Koala Lou, I DO love you! I always have, and I always will.'

And she hugged her for a very long time.

For Lailu and Jan — M.F.
For Mum and for Gaby — P.L.

UK | USA | Canada | Ireland | Australia
India | New Zealand | South Africa | China

Penguin Books is part of the Penguin Random House group of companies
whose addresses can be found at global.penguinrandomhouse.com.

 Penguin
Random House
Australia

First published in Great Britain by Viking, 1989
First Puffin edition published by Penguin Books Australia Ltd, 1991
This edition Published by Penguin Group (Australia), 2010

Printed in China
National Library of Australia Cataloguing-in-Publication data available.
ISBN 978 0 14 350516 7
penguin.com.au